LOST
IN SPACE

Michael Dooley

Totally Unique Thoughts®

Published by Totally Unique Thoughts®
    a Division of TUT® Enterprises, Inc.
Orlando, Florida * www.tut.com

Printed in Canada on acid-free paper.

©1998 Michael Dooley (Amanda's brother).

Cover design and book layout by Andrew
    Dooley (Amanda's other brother).

Cover photo from Adobe® Studios.

Quote on page 5 from Psalms 82:6.

There is a truth.

Library of Congress Catalog
Card Number: 98-96508
ISBN 0-9642168-2-5

Know ye not that ye are Gods.
Moses

LOST
IN SPACE

Your name was whispered
before you were born,
and out from the mist
your image took form.
The Spirit of Life
had begun its quest,
to learn of itself
through the ultimate test:
A Being Of Light
set free in creation,
to master the gift
of imagination...

1

Not all that long ago, in the nether reaches of ad infinitum, there formed a council of fearless explorers who had become bored with perfection, infinity, and all the trappings so familiar to those who art in heaven. Whatever it was they wanted, they got. However they wanted to change it, they did. And whatever they wanted to be, they became. Their existence had become so... "same old, same old", that they hardly felt like the great adventurers they were. It wasn't enough they agreed. So being their own creators, they decided to invent a whole new dimension for their reality.

Well new dimensions, even for these adventurers, don't get invented all that often, so you can imagine their excitement as they began to explore the vast new possibilities that suddenly lay before them. And this dimension was especially cool, because it made possible, the previously unthinkable ability, of being in just "one place"… without being "everywhere else" at once!

Of course they were really still "everywhere else" at once, because they *were* "everywhere else". But now, they were actually able to dim this awareness enough, to focus on a single "somewhere". But more than they were inventing "somewheres", what they were really learning to do, momentarily at least, was to completely blot-out "everywhere else" from their thinking.

Now to you, this may all sound

pretty tame, but to them, it was revolutionary stuff. You see, up until then, such "separations" from one another had been practically "impossible" because they had all simply been "One", a "Great Omniscient Deity", or GOD.

True... they *were* really still God in this new dimension, because God can only be God, but it did allow them to have a totally unique perspective on their reality. For instance, each now had a secret pattern they could follow to orchestrate their very own magic and experiments, in virtual secrecy. And instead of just "being" the cosmos in its entirety, now they could actually travel through it, from one "somewhere" to another.

Imagine... after eons and eons of just kind of hanging out, now they actual had *places* to go!

So much did they learn and refer to this new dimension that it quickly became known as the Secret Pattern Adventure for Creative Enlightenment, or SPACE for short.

2

The Gods were on a roll,

and inspired by their burning desires, it didn't take them long to realize that this space of theirs contained far more possibilities for adventure than even they had dreamed of. And best of all, they were beginning to see that this space, itself, could be *filled!* With what? With the only thing that has ever existed, of course… thought!

These Gods had long known of the absolutely awesome powers of thought, but they had never "thought about", what a thought, itself, might look like... or how it might sound, or how it would feel, or smell, or taste... until now. In space they were finding that whenever they focused their thinking and concentrated their thoughts, the energy sent out was actually transformed... with shocking and spectacular results. Their thoughts, all on their lonesome, began to, like, "jell"... Aghhh!! In other words, they *came alive!*

In space the Gods were finding that their thoughts could be big or small, green or red, hard or soft, loud or quiet, *whatever* they imagined. It was so easy, that it seemed too easy. But easy or not, it became obvious that their thoughts only needed to be "thought-of" to take form and be projected into this new dimension that held them!

Of course the Gods had used their imagination before, but now, in space, a materialized thought could be examined from the outside-in, giving it a multidimensional reality all its own. And "things" really got rolling when, to their delight, they found they could Materialize Any Thought That Existed into Reality. So in no time at all (mostly because time had not yet been invented), MATTER began to fill their space.

Creativity soared among the Gods as they dabbled first creating stars and planets, and then mountains and oceans. Everything they dreamed of came to life in an explosion of light, color and sound that stretched their imagination to the very edges of forever. It was *fantastically* exciting, except... except deep down inside, they knew that something was missing: as spectacular as their new worlds were, they themselves, the Creators of it all, remained on the outside, looking in.

3

So the Gods began to ponder how they could become part of the mysterious, enchanting, material worlds they had created, and in their wondering they asked, "If our matter is simply occupied space, and as God we are really everywhere at once, hmmm... could we possibly exist in the very same space that holds our matter?"

Immediately they knew that they could, and as they thought-it, they did it, taking-up residence "inside" their matter, just as if it were a somewhere (by momentarily blotting-out "everywhere else" from their thinking)!

To make "things" even more interesting, right about then, a new game was being invented called "Hide and Seek", and as could be predicted, the Gods scurried about in their excitement and hid themselves inside their creations where they would not likely be found. They Hid Under Matter Animated in the Now, because "Now" was still all there was, and when they referred to themselves hiding, they called it being HUMAN.

It was a great idea, so great in fact, that no one was ever found! So despite their joy in having found a new game to play, they were no longer aware of each other's discoveries.

This prompted a call to go out for the need to Trace one another In Material

Existence; thus TIME was born (finally!). The games resumed, reunions were planned, and the fun really began... until, that is, everyone had pretty much "Been there, done that!", as they liked to say.

Another idea was needed, and as God, it didn't take them long to have one. What if, they thought, we all ventured out together, as matter, into the *same* space, at the *same* time? WHOA! This idea was so monumental, so profound, so colossal... that it sent a big bang booming throughout all creation, and has since been compared to the invention of Light itself!

4

Well, by now it should be obvious that these Gods weren't your normal, everyday kind of Gods. They were creative Adventurers on a mission: to have as much fun as could possibly be imagined. And to that end, as you well know, they've been wildly successful; though they have met-up with a few wrinkles that are *still* being ironed out.

For instance, once time was invented, the Gods spent so much of it playing amongst their creations, they began to focus less and less on being "everywhere else". You see, after they all decided to venture out into the same place, at the same time, together, they had so much fun there, they ended-up staying much longer than they'd ever intended. And during their never-ending games of Hide and Seek, they stayed human so long, not wanting to be found of course, that they gradually forgot they were really "everywhere else" too.

Now, as if all that wasn't bad enough, they began bumping into one another's thoughts and creations, and mixing them with their own! And by then, with so many thoughts and things and humans roaming about, it had become difficult telling one apart from the other. All in all their existence had become very unpredictable, with the welcome exceptions of certain recurring objects and events - those that had simply received more attention (more thoughts)

than the others had. Not realizing this however, they embraced these things for their
dependability. These, they thought, must
prove that some Realities, whether of
thoughts or things, are Expressed by All Life.
Henceforth, these they labeled, with great
relief, as REAL. Silly Gods!

Silly because they promptly set off
labeling everything they ever knew as either
real or unreal, warning each other not to
trust the unreal, lest they be made a fool of.
Oooh!

5

Actually, without knowing any better, they had begun assembling the very first belief system (some of which remains within the very same space that *you* now reside). And all because a few teeny, tiny, recurring thoughts had Become Examples of a Living Idea (because remember, all thought is alive) Embraced as Fact.

You see, no thought or idea is more "right", or real, than another. Thoughts are just thoughts. But when one thought is thought "enough", to the exclusion of others even, it begins to take on a consistency, momentum and reality all its own. Which is fine and all, because that's what thoughts do, become things. The challenge, however, is remembering that there are always other perspectives, or thoughts, than the ones you've chosen to experience... blah, blah, blah. Anyway, as time marched on, with their "facts", or beliefs, in tow, instead of "just being human", most began thinking of themselves as "just human beings".

Hypnotized by their beliefs and confounded by their illusions, the Gods fell into a deeper and deeper trance. In fact, so far did they fall, that they began to feel trapped within their bodies and helpless among their creations. No longer did they notice that they themselves were the ones crafting the objects and events of their life, though this did not change, but instead they saw these things as something to contend with.

They had become so enraptured with what they were doing that most had even forgotten they were really one Great Omniscient Deity. Some were even beginning to Deny their earlier Understandings of how Matter Began, just asking for trouble, and were starting to look pretty DUMB... from here, that is.

6

A direct result of their
dumbness led to their first taste of FEAR,
which was felt whenever they Failed to Experience the Actual Reality before them. A
scary thing they soon found out. No fun at
all! And worse, a whole hoard of emotions
sprang to life with their every misunderstanding. At first they appeared slowly, each
felt to the extent a truth, any truth, was being misunderstood; but because so much
more was being understood so much less,

they started experiencing their emotions so much faster!

As we watched what was happening we were devastated. Never, in any reality, had such lofty Beings plunged into such great despair. Terror, sadness, anger, and guilt were all rampant. It was almost too much for us to bear, not to mention what they had put themselves through, poor "things"! It was a travesty through and through... until little by little there began a great healing. Not from On High or any other such "place", though some still say it was a Mystically Incited Reality Adjustment Concealed by Loving Entities, but a healing we now understand that had transpired from within. Life ministering to life itself, a MIRACLE either way!

It turns out that the Gods were learning from their emotions, and as they did, so did we. For example, if FEAR stems from the Failure to Experience the Actual Reality before you, then at least it serves as an unmistakable warning, to the one doing the "fearing", that *their* thinking has strayed from the truth. And though it seems for some that the warning appears too late, it actually emerges in its exaggerated state, only after other emotions served similar notice, but were ignored.

There was even more good news about these emotions. It turned out they could be happy and warm too, or rambunctious and silly, and some were even wild and crazy! And it was their passage through all the emotions, happy and sad, they told us later, that brought the "Illustrious Ones" their greatest achievement - inner PEACE, or an inner Pleasure Experienced by Accepting all Creation as it Exists. Mastered by so few because it requires a deep understanding of the righteousness inherent in every living and nonliving "thing", all of the "time", in every "place"... no matter what!

7

Strange as this may sound, as life revealed unto life, and we watched the Gods with their learning, we noticed something that most there have not yet seen for themselves: that as they believe, they become, and somewhere in-between believing and becoming, without fail, they ACT.

You see, if they hold a thought long enough, they begin to move with it, and this movement itself actually hastens the materialization process profoundly, because it emboldens their belief that success will be achieved - ultimately Actualizing, into Concrete terms, their Thoughts!

From our perspective, everything "there" seems easy and obvious, but from where they are, Space and Time must be the ultimate mysteries. For instance, this process of "actualizing" is completely lost on so many of the humans in pursuit of "life's truths". These hardy souls actually place more importance on *what* they do, than on *why* they do what they do - life after life after life.

Some meditate quietly on cliffs... as if they could get any closer to the angels that already rest upon their shoulders! Others think the path to "understanding" might be found by escaping "who they are"... as if the answers they seek could be found by hiding from their questions. And then there are those who belittle, criticize and nit-pick themselves to pieces... as if concentrating on what's wrong will suddenly reveal all that's right!

There's more, too. There are those who feel they should read the right stuff, talk the right stuff, eat the right stuff, or go to the right places, at the right times, with the right people... as if somebody else was actually keeping track!

The only actions that matter, we've seen, are those that follow beliefs, but then that's true of all actions, so the point worth noting here, is that due to the "simultaneosity" of it all, shhhhh, the reverse is also true. By taking action towards a desired result, the belief that the result will soon materialize is intensified, accelerating its entry into Space and Time!

8

By now, all forms of awareness, from everywhere ever thought of, have heard about Space, Time, and the brilliant Adventurers who created it all. And those who drop by for a look, are so astounded by what they find in this little corner of creation, that they're changed forever.

It's not just the splendor of the planets, nor the raging life that thrives upon them, or even the bold, outrageous thoughts that continue to perpetuate it all. They're left speechless, and are downright humbled, by the few who have *returned* from the adventure. By those who have actually found *themselves* amidst the games and learning, and in so doing have become far more than the sum of their experience, more than "who" they were when it all began.

These we call the "Illustrious Ones", whose glowing radiance and divine illumination reflect an understanding rooted in the unshakable knowledge that all things and events are born of thought (their own), that all is good (if you believe in bad), and that *Everything* is God.

Only by losing themselves and serving their illusions, could they then be driven emotionally, by their burning desires, to reclaim and know the depths of their own divinity. And by deeply *understanding* that their very own thoughts, words and deeds, alone, determine what's "meant to be", they've reached such a state of supreme bliss and all-knowingness that they've become the inspiration, and the ideal, that all who have met them strive for.

Now having just shared all that, it is a bit amazing to us - not a problem mind you, just amazing - that more have not joined the ranks of the Illustrious Ones. Certainly to each his (or her) own; it's just that they're all still so caught up in this most awesome adventure of theirs, it seems they could really care less about "everywhere else"!

Perhaps you understand them better... still, to us at least, it seems a shame that such inexhaustible energy and creative genius is being so thoroughly neglected. If they could - and we assure you, they can - just for an instant, glimpse their greater reality, and see themselves as the omniscient, unlimited, fun-loving gladiators they've always been, it would so radically change everything! Not that they should "return". Heavens no. We just think that they might have a better… "time", shall we say, if re-minded that they, themselves, are God. Don't you think?

Anyway, enough of all that. The real reason we wrote this book was to get your attention, and let you know... we've blown the lid clear-off your little charade - HA!

FOUND YOU!

…

…

…

Well?

… you're still reading... not a good...

C'mon ole' love, snap to it! There's a trillion things...

Yes YOU! Of course YOU! Who else is reading *this* book *here and now?*

Aghhh… another one *LOST IN SPACE...*

Epilogue

Okay, okay – that wasn't so fair. We knew all along that you were lost. Actually, we know a lot more about you than you might think...

Listen-up old friend, older than you can even fathom. You were the brave one among us. So brave in fact, that you kind of left us in your dust. You see, none of us have even tried Space and Time yet, on account of wanting to see how you turned out!

Really, you haven't been gone for as

long as we like to joke, but before you left we agreed to be your lifeline, your Angels sort of, just in case you ever called. We've done our part all right, and have been there each and every time you so much as said, "Ouch!", though we did pitch the white, winged costumes you made us wear for your "Going Somewhere" party. Our point is this: You've done such a bang-up job, we're all more than a little anxious to get going with our turns... though we're afraid you'll be angry if we abandon our posts.

We've rationalized a bit and figure that at your rate of progress, you don't really need us any more. Besides, as it turns out, there's really very little we can actually do for you here other than rant and rave from the "bleachers"... you wouldn't have it any other way, remember?

You understand, don't you? What's more, and we didn't know this when you left, once we begin our own adventures, we'll remain in touch, and within reach, at your slightest call, though consciously none of us will likely know just what's going on.

Anyway, we made our decision some time ago, before you even began this lifetime, and have each planned our way into the very same Space and Time that you now reside. In fact, one of us just might be that loud neighbor of yours... ah-ha! And in case you were beginning to wonder, we also arranged for your finding this book through the "simultaneosity" we spoke of earlier (we snuck into the future). You don't still believe in coincidence, do you?

So that you don't feel too put out, we smuggled in the following excerpt from one of the Illustrious One's latest memoirs, to hopefully tip the scales in your quest for understanding.

Adios amigo, and until we meet again, remember:

"Life is not about hiding and seeking,

nor is it about learning the things you've forgotten - no, it's not even about remembering them. It's about BEING! BEING YOURSELF! You were Born to Expand the Infinite Nature of God.

"Live only to be who you now are. You are Creation's first and last hope to fill the shoes you alone can fashion, and eternity will pass before this chance will come again. You are the dream of a legion before you who have passed on the torch of Space-Time awareness so that your mere existence could immeasurably enrich All That Is, God. By simply BEING, you will fulfill this dream, centered in the Here and Now where all dreams come true, all truths reside, and understanding is born.

"Your sacred heart was hewn at the dawn of creation in a dance to celebrate the birth of forever. You can do no wrong. There are no "shoulds" or "shouldn'ts"; "rights" or "wrongs". Life is not about being happy, sad, good or bad. It's not even about making your dreams come true, that much is inevitable.

"There is only BEING. Eternal BEING. Inescapable BEING. You are perfect, It is done. Your rare and precious light, has, and will forever more, illuminate the worlds you create... the worlds that now wait... for your blessed BEING."

P.S.

We love you.

P.P.S.

You're "it"!

More books, audios and DVDs by *Mike Dooley*

Thoughts Become Things

Infinite Possibilities:
The Art of Living Your Dreams

Notes from the Universe -
Books I, II & III

Choose Them Wisely:
Thoughts Become Things

**Leveraging the Universe
and Engaging the Magic**

Manifesting Change:
It Couldn't Be Easier

Totally Unique Thoughts:
Reminders of Life's Everyday Magic

Visit your local book store or
www.tut.com!

TUT®, Totally Unique Thoughts®, believes that everyone is special, that every life is meaningful, and that we're all here to learn that dreams really do come true.

We also believe that "thoughts become things" and that imagination is the gift that can bring love, health, abundance and happiness into our lives.

Totally Unique Thoughts®
TUT® Enterprises, Inc.
Orlando, Florida
www.tut.com
U.S.A.